A Slimy Story

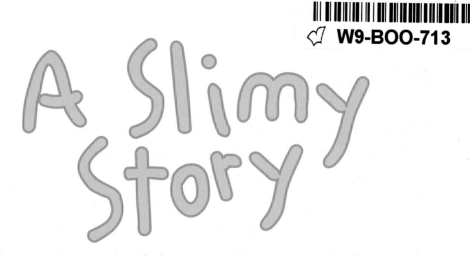

by Michelle Knudsen
illustrated by Paige Billin-Frye

The Kane Press
New York

Acknowledgements: Our thanks to Mary Appelhof , M.S. in Biological Sciences and M.S. in Education (Michigan State University), author of *Worms Eat My Garbage* (Flower Press, Kalamazoo, Michigan, rev. ed. 1997) for helping us make this book as accurate as possible.

To learn more about worms and the environment, visit www.wormwoman.com.

Library of Congress Cataloging-in-Publication Data

Knudsen, Michelle.
  A slimy story / by Michelle Knudsen ; illustrated by Paige Billin-Frye.
     p. cm. — (Science solves it!)
  Summary: When Dan accidentally brings an earthworm to school, he gets a homework assignment that helps him solve a nagging problem—what to give his mother for her birthday.
  ISBN 1-57565-144-0 (pbk. : alk. paper)
  [1. Earthworms—Fiction. 2. Gifts—Fiction. 3. Schools—Fiction.] I. Billin-Frye, Paige, ill. II. Title. III. Series.
  PZ7.K7835Sli 2004
  [E]—dc22

                                                      2004001324

10 9 8 7 6 5 4 3 2 1
First published in the United States of America in 2004 by The Kane Press.
Printed in Hong Kong.

Science Solves It! is a registered trademark of The Kane Press.

Book Design/Art Direction: Edward Miller

www.kanepress.com

I have a big problem.

Mom's surprise birthday party is only a few days away. And what do I have to give her for a present?

Nothing, that's what.

I'm trying to make a list of gift ideas. So far, all I have written is "Gift Ideas." The rest of the page is blank.

The door to my room flies open. "Hey, Dan," says my big brother, Todd. "Check out what I got Mom for her birthday! Gardening gloves!"

I'm impressed. Mom loves gardening. "Cool idea," I say, trying to sound happy.

Inside, I don't feel happy at all. Todd has been saving up for weeks, so he can afford a great gift. I haven't saved anything.

The World's Best Gardening Gloves

The next morning is gray and rainy. My friend Stacey is waiting at the corner. We always walk to school together.

I open my mouth to say hello.

"Stop!" Stacey shouts. "Don't move!"

I freeze. "Why? What's wrong?"

"You almost stepped on that earthworm!" she says, pointing to the ground.

There are about 5,000 different kinds of earthworms in the world.

I roll my eyes. But I wait while she rescues the soggy little creature.

"Look, there are more," says Stacey. "Help me move them into the grass."

"No way!" I say. "I'm not touching those slimy things." I look at one of the worms. It's long and pinkish. I can't tell which end is the head and which is the tail.

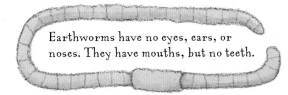

Earthworms have no eyes, ears, or noses. They have mouths, but no teeth.

"What have you got against earthworms?" asks Stacey. "I think they're neat."

"I think they're slimy, squishy, and gross," I say. "And you're weird."

"Are you in a bad mood or something?" Stacey asks.

"Sorry," I say. "My mom's birthday is in two days and I don't have a gift for her—or enough money to get one."

"You'll think of something," Stacey says.

I hope she's right.

Earthworms are squishy because they have no bones! Worms are a kind of animal called **invertebrates.** Invertebrates do not have backbones.

Gift Ideas
1. Learn to knit and make her socks.
2. Bake a cake and jump out of it.
3. Gardening stuff????

During lunch, I jot down a few gift ideas. They are all pretty bad.

I groan and put my head down on my notebook. This is hopeless!

There are more worms on the sidewalk the next morning. Yuck! But I step carefully so I won't squish any of them.

Todd sneaks up on me. "What's wrong, Dan? Afraid of touching a little worm?"

He dangles one right in my face.

"Why would I be afraid of worms?" I ask him.
"They're not nearly as gross as *you* are."
I walk off before he can say anything else.

Why do earthworms come up out of the ground when it rains? Some scientists believe the worms are looking for mates. But others don't agree on what the real reason is. It's a wormy mystery!

When we get to class, Stacey pulls me aside. "Um . . . Dan? Do you know there's a worm in your pocket?"

A little pink head—or maybe a tail—is poking out of my jacket pocket. "Oh, gross," I say. "That stupid Todd. He must have stuck the worm in there when my back was turned."

Some other kids notice the worm, too.

"Eww!" says Amanda. "Why did you bring a worm to school?"

"Gross!" says Andy.

"What's going on back here?" asks Ms. Stewart.

"Dan brought a worm to school!" says Amanda.

"New friend, Dan?" asks Ms. Stewart.

"More like a stowaway," I say.

Ms. Stewart laughs. "Well, since it's here, it might as well stay awhile. But it'll need a better place to hang out."

"How about this jar?" asks Stacey. "I'll put in some dirt and old leaves from the window plants."

"Perfect," says Ms. Stewart.

Is Dan's worm a he or a she? Neither. Worms are **hermaphrodites** (her-MA-fruh-dites). That means they have both male and female parts.

I pick up the worm. It isn't really *that* gross, but I still don't like touching it. I drop it into the jar. The worm starts moving slowly on top of the dirt.

Worms need moist soil in order to breathe. Air and water from the soil pass through a worm's slimy skin and into its body.

Everyone stands around looking at it.
"What's the worm doing?" asks Amanda.
"Do worms have brains?" asks Peter.
"Can we name it Wiggler?" asks Stacey.
"Which end is the head?" I ask. I still can't tell.

How do worms get around without arms or legs? Earthworms have special muscles and bristles (called **setae**) that help them move through the dirt.

17

Ms. Stewart smiles. "Why don't you all look up some facts about earthworms for homework tonight? Then we can share them tomorrow."

She picks up the worm jar. "For now, let's give our worm some time to get used to its new home."

Earthworms like the dark. Even though they can't see, they can sense light. If you shine a light on a worm, it will try to dig, hide, or move away.

Stacey drags me to the library after school.
"I need to be thinking of gift ideas," I complain.
"Mom's party is tomorrow. Besides, this is going
to be so boring."

But once we start looking through some books, a funny thing happens. I forget to be bored. Worms are actually interesting!

Pretty soon Stacey and I are telling each other all kinds of weird worm facts. I even discover how to tell the head from the tail!

That night I decide I have to face the truth.
I'm not going to come up with a good present
for Mom by tomorrow. There is only one thing
to do. It's kind of lame, but it's still better than
nothing.

I.O.U
One Present

Happy Birthday,
Mom!
Love, Dan

The next morning Ms. Stewart brings out the worm jar.

"Wiggler made tunnels in the dirt!" says Sue.

"Worms *eat* dirt," says Peter.

"And they're covered with snot," says Andy.

"It's called *mucus*," says Stacey.

Earthworms belong to the Annelid family. An annelid's body is made up of segments.

Jobs for Different Worms

Close Up of an Earthworm's Mou

Peter

"And they help plants," says Amanda. "Because they air—airy—"

"Aerate the soil?" asks Ms. Stewart.

"Yes. What you said," says Amanda. "They're good for gardens."

An Earthworm's Body

Anus

Setae (Bristles)

Segment

Clitellum

Mouth

The clitellum makes a cocoon for the earthworm's eggs.

Stacey

Earthworms are like underground farmers. Their tunnels help air and water get down into the soil.

Good for gardens, I think. I look down at my list of worm facts. My gift ideas are on the other page. I look back and forth between the two lists.

Gift Ideas
1. Learn to knit and make her socks.
2. Bake a cake and jump out of it.
3. Gardening stuff????

Facts About Earthworms

1. Birds eat earthworms and so do moles.
2. If certain kinds of earthworms lose their tails, they can sometimes grow new ones.
3. Cutting a worm in half does not make two worms!
4. Earthworms help plants grow better.

"That's it!" I shout.
Everyone turns to stare at me.

"Worms would make a great gift for someone who's a gardener!" I say. I look up at the teacher. "Wouldn't they?"

"I'd have to agree with that," Ms. Stewart says. "A pretty original gift, too!"

Way to go, Dan!

Some kinds of worms are great recyclers! Some people even keep worm bins. They put in food scraps and other garbage. The worms eat the garbage and leave behind castings (poop) that can be added to gardens as fertilizer.

Stacey helps me dig up some earthworms from her backyard after school. I let her do most of the actual worm touching. Maybe worms *are* neat, but they are still kind of icky.

We put all the worms in a jar. It's almost time for the party.

"You'd better get going," Stacey says. "Good luck!"

I hurry home. When I reach my house, I cover the jar with my jacket and sneak up to my room.

I wrap up the worms and make it downstairs just in time. Mom is coming in the front door. "SURPRISE!" we all shout.

Soon it's time to open the presents. Mom gets lots of great stuff. And she *loves* Todd's gardening gloves.

Mine is the only gift left to open. I'm excited. And a little nervous.

Mom tears off the wrapping paper. "What's that?" someone whispers. "*Worms?*"

Uh-oh, I think. Maybe this wasn't such a good idea after all.

"Earthworms for my garden!" Mom says. "What a great gift!" She gives me a big hug.

So everything turned out really great. But I just can't help wondering about one thing. What do I give Mom *next* year?

THINK LIKE A SCIENTIST

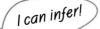

Dan thinks like a scientist—and so can you!

Scientists infer. They use what they see or observe to help explain why or how something happens. You infer, too. Suppose you see a group of people with balloons and presents. You might infer that they are going to a party.

Look Back

What earthworm fact does Amanda mention on page 23? Look at Dan's list on page 24. Which fact is most like Amanda's? Using this information, what does Dan infer on page 25?

Try This!

Look closely at the pictures. What do you observe? What can you infer?

1.   2.   3.

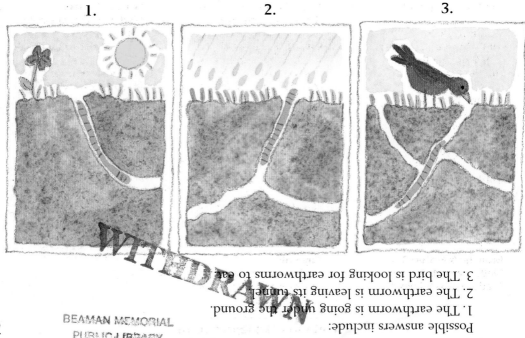

Possible answers include:
1. The earthworm is going under the ground.
2. The earthworm is leaving its tunnel.
3. The bird is looking for earthworms to eat.